D1273059

Reycraft Books
55 Fifth Avenue
New York, NY 10003

Reycraftbooks.com

Reycraft Books is a trade imprint and trademark of Newmark Learning, LLC.

This edition is published by arrangement with China Children's Press & Publication Group, China.
© China Children's Press & Publication Group

All rights reserved. No portion of this book may be reproduced, stored in a retrieval
system, or transmitted in any form or by any means, electronic, mechanical, photocopying,
recording, or otherwise, without written permission from the publisher. For information regarding
permission, please contact info@reycraftbooks.com.

Educators and Librarians: Our books may be purchased in bulk for promotional, educational,
or business use. Please contact sales@reycraftbooks.com.

This is a work of fiction. Names, characters, places, dialogue, and incidents described either are the
product of the author's imagination or are used fictitiously. Any resemblance to actual
persons, living or dead, is entirely coincidental.

Sale of this book without a front cover or jacket may be unauthorized. If this book is
coverless, it may have been reported to the publisher as "unsold or destroyed" and may have
deprived the author and publisher of payment.

Library of Congress Cataloging-in-Publication Data is available.

ISBN: 978-1-4788-6932-0
Printed in Guangzhou, China
4401/0120/CA22000033

10 9 8 7 6 5 4 3 2 1

First Edition Hardcover published by Reycraft Books 2020

Reycraft Books and Newmark Learning, LLC, support diversity and
the First Amendment, and celebrate the right to read.

Ant in a Book

by Yimei Wang
illustrated by Cao Cao

Chinese writing uses
characters, not letters.
The characters stand for
words and parts of words.

WITHDRAWN

FREMONT PUBLIC LIBRARY DISTRICT
1170 N. Midlothian Road
Mundelein, IL 60060

A little red flower stood

alone in an age-old corner,

gently singing

in the wind.

A little ant **climbed up the stalk**

...and slept quietly in the petals.

A little girl came,
plucked the flower,
and put it

inside an old book.

Oops!
The little ant also went
into the book and was
flattened.

When the now-flat
little ant woke,
he heard softly
murmuring voices.

The little ant was surprised.

"Who are YOU? I didn't know books could talk."

"We're characters,"

the soft voices murmured.

Not until then did the ant
see that the book was
packed with them.

"We're like little ants,"
the characters said shyly.

借着萤火虫的亮
的路到了回家

我们到处找你，你去哪里了？

"Well, I'm flat now, so I guess I'm like a character," said the little ant.

如果风一直吹⋯⋯

"But I can move.
I'm like a moving
character."

So on the first day, the ant hung out on page 100.

On the next day,

he moved to page 50.

And on the third day, he moved on to page 200.

别人都很羡
我这条项链.

很快，蚂蚁找来了梯子。

The characters were amazed.

After all, it was a very old book and it had been ages since someone flipped through it. These characters had never thought of moving around.

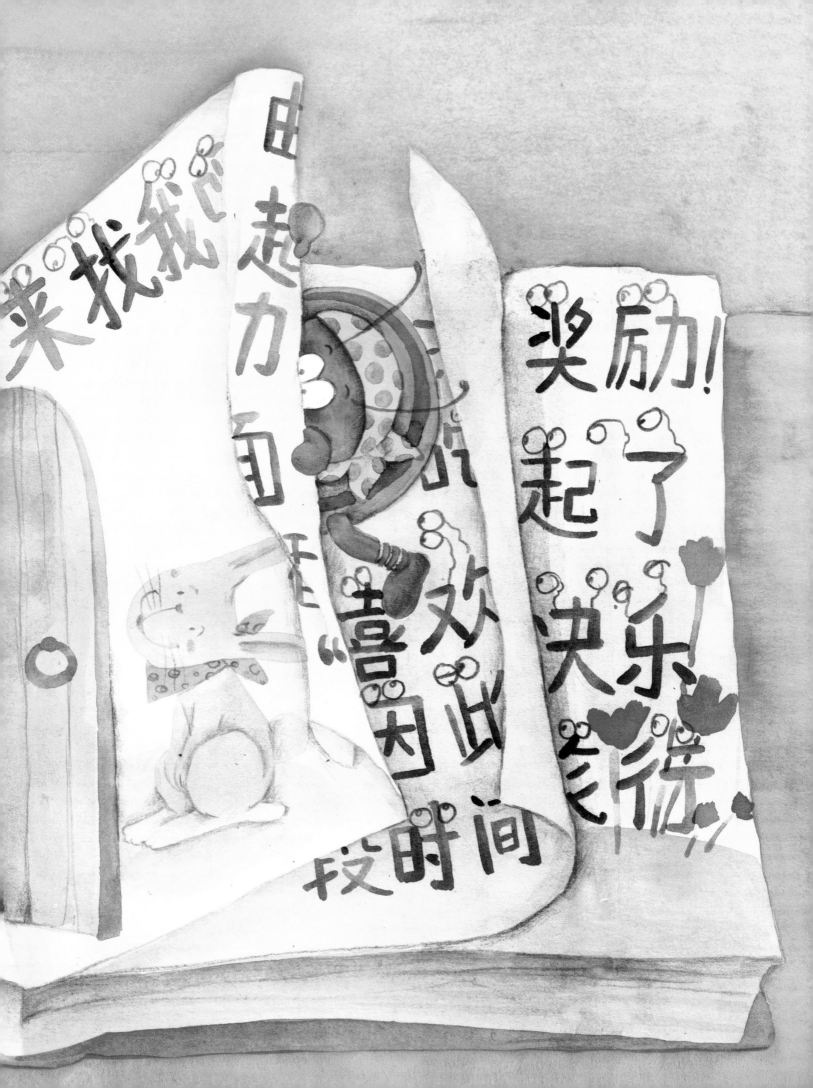

"Silly us for not thinking of that!"

the characters said.

They began following the ant, dancing around from page to page.

And the old book **began to change.**

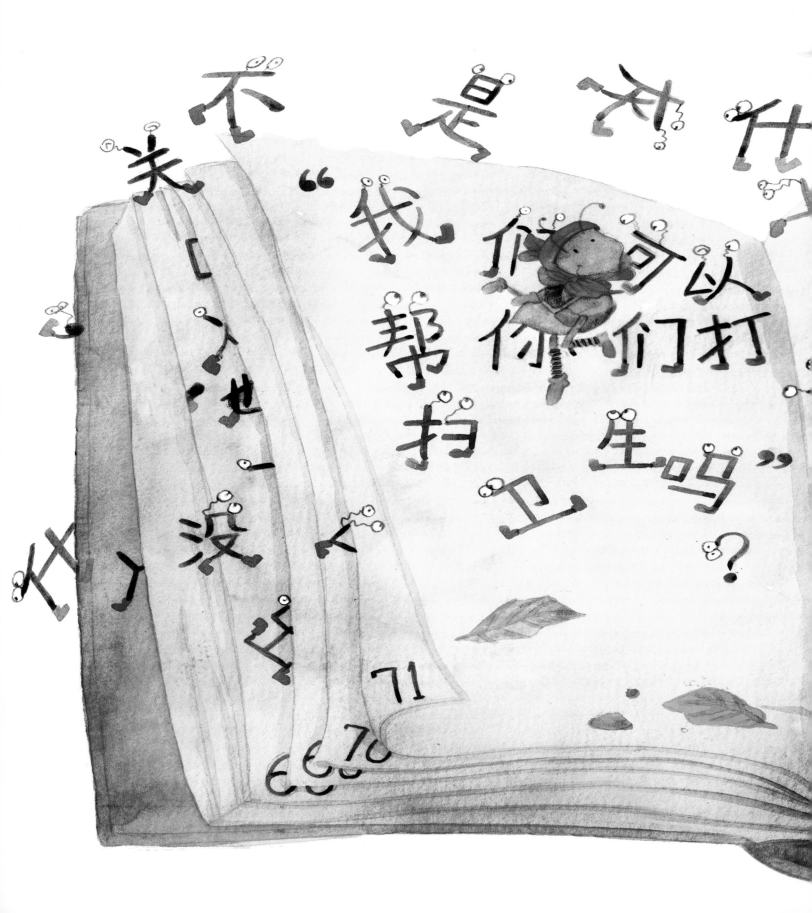

One day, the little girl remembered the beautiful flower and opened the book.

Ah! She had read this old book many times, but now the story was completely new.

She devoured it in one sitting.

The next day, the little girl couldn't
help but open the book again. She was
amazed to see another new story.

Then the little girl saw the flat little ant.

"Are you a character in my book?" she asked.

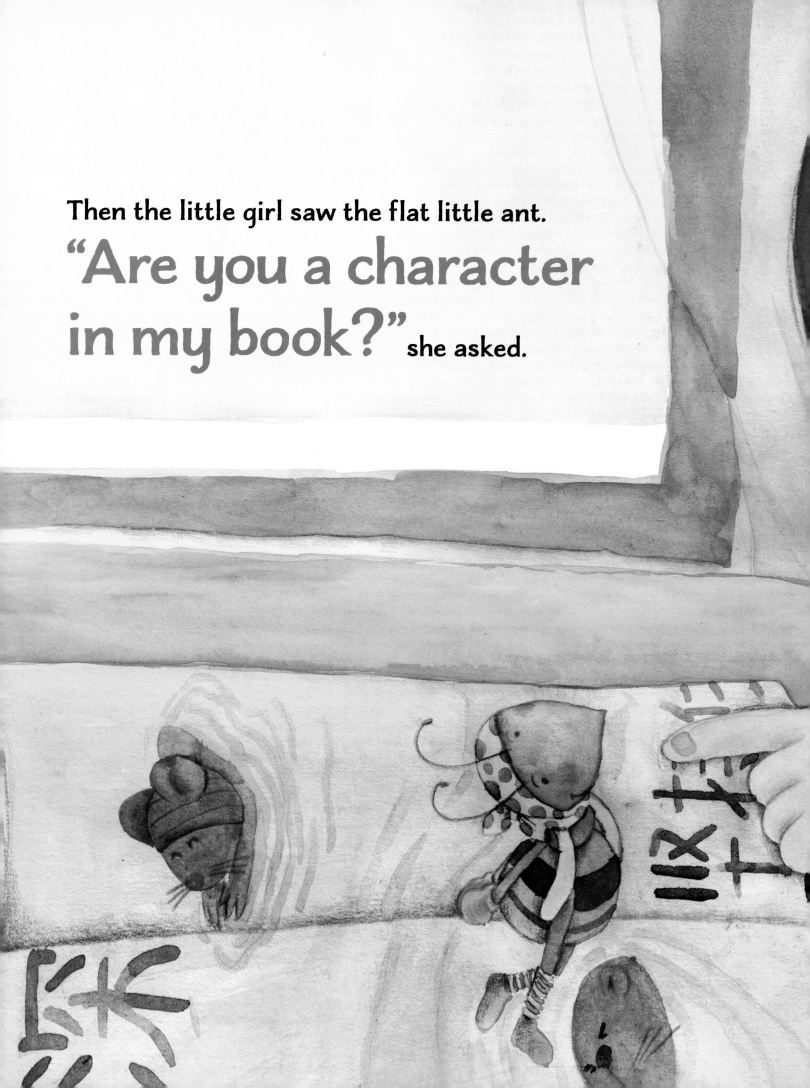

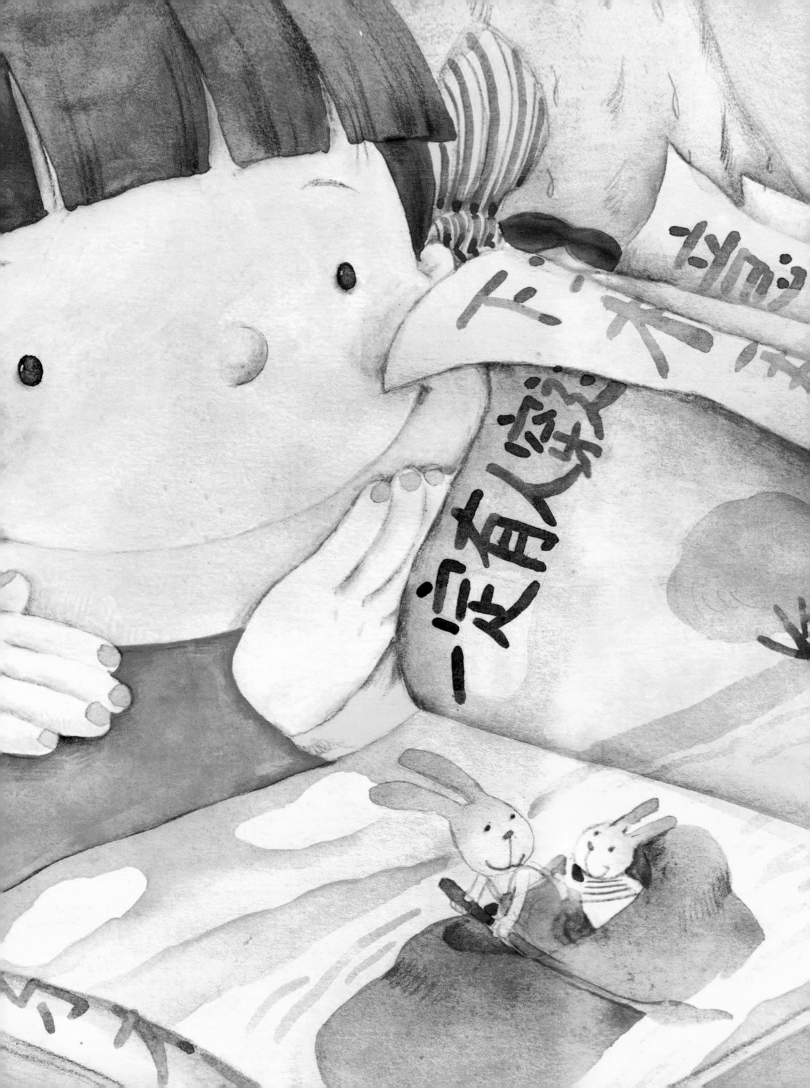

"Yes. I used to
be a little ant.
But now I live in this book."

And the flat ant ran
across the pages.

The little girl suddenly realized what had happened. The characters in the book jumped around every night, so the story kept changing.

On the third morning, the girl found
a character on the book's cover.

"Where are you going?" she asked.

"I want to leave the book and see the world," he said.

But none of the other characters wanted to leave the book.

They lived together happily
ever after, making a new
story each day.

And the little girl started
each morning by reading it.

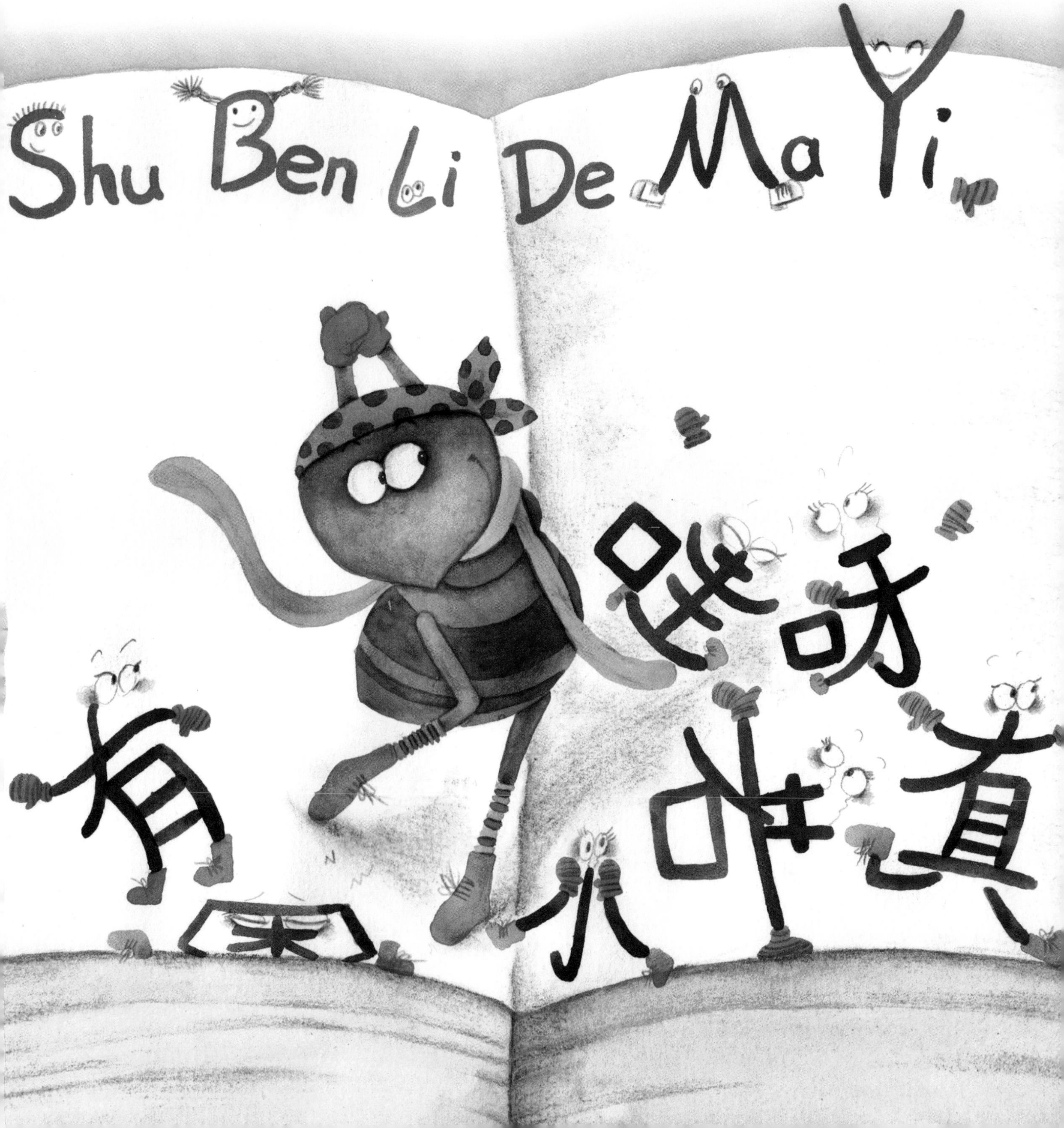
Shu Ben Li De Ma Yi